You're FIRED!

Based on the teleplay by Marc Ceccarelli, Luke Brookshier, and Mr. Lawrence
Illustrated by Dave Aikins

A Random House PICTUREBACK® Book

Random House 🏠 **New York**

created by

Stephen Hillenburg

randomhouse.com/kids

ISBN 978-0-385-37431-6

Printed in the United States of America

10 9 8 7 6 5 4 3 2

It was a busy day at the Krusty Krab—and SpongeBob loved every minute of it! He mopped the floors and the ceiling, washed the dishes, and cooked some Krabby Patties.

"There's nothing better than a perfect Krabby Patty served in a squeaky-clean Krusty Krab," he declared. "I love my job!"

Just then, Mr. Krabs stepped out of his office.

"Hi, Mr. Krabs! What's the good word?" SpongeBob asked.

"Well, there are two words," Mr. Krabs replied. "And they're not very good: You're fired."

"Wh-wh-what?" SpongeBob sputtered.

"If I cut your job," Mr. Krabs explained, "I can save a whole nickel!"

SpongeBob was so shocked, he couldn't move. Squidward loaded him onto a cart and rolled him out the door.

"Bye-bye," Squidward said. "Please visit soon . . . as a customer."

That night, Patrick heard moaning coming from SpongeBob's house. He stopped by to see what was wrong.

"It's terrible!" SpongeBob cried. "I got f-f . . . f-f . . ."

"Did you get free french fries?" Patrick asked. "A frothy frappe?"

"No, Patrick, I got fired!" SpongeBob wailed.
"Don't worry," Patrick said. "Starting tomorrow,
I'll teach you the wonders of FUN-employment!"

SpongeBob and Patrick started their day by standing in
Squidward's garden and waving at him.
"Stay off my petunias!" Squidward yelled, throwing vegetables.
Splat! Splat!
"I call this free breakfast," said Patrick, licking tomatoes off his face.

Later that day, SpongeBob and Patrick went to Sandy's for free lunch. Little did they know, the food was really a science experiment—with weird side effects.

"This is delicious," Patrick declared.

"More! More!" demanded the little face that popped out of Patrick's forehead.

"SpongeBob, you look terrible!" Sandy exclaimed. She warned SpongeBob not to eat the food. "What you need is to clean up, get a routine, and find a new job!"

SpongeBob knew Sandy was right. "I'm ready!" he shouted. "I'm ready to find a new job!"

SpongeBob thought he could get another job as a fry cook, so he went to the Weenie Hut. The manager hired him right away, but SpongeBob didn't like the kitchen. They didn't use a grill to cook the hot dogs. They used a strange rolling machine.

"This isn't right," SpongeBob said to himself. He grabbed a spatula, used it to dice a few cooked hot dogs and buns, and made—Weenie Patties! "You're fired," the manager said.

Everywhere SpongeBob went, it was the same story. At the Pizza Piehole, they didn't like his Pizza Patties.

At the Taco Sombrero, his Burrito Patty squirted beans everywhere.

And he was kicked out of the Wet Noodle
because his Noodle Patties were a mess.

When SpongeBob got home, he was really depressed.
"I've been fired five times," he sighed. "At least you still
like my cooking, Gary."
Just then, there was a knock at the front door.

SpongeBob opened the door to find two big
men dressed as hot dogs! They shoved him into
a giant bun and ran away with him.

SpongeBob was taken to the Weenie Hut and chained to the hot dog cooker. The manager apologized for firing him. "But that's all mustard under the bun now, right? What's important is that my customers love your Weenie Patties! GET TO WORK!" the manager ordered, then marched out of the kitchen.

"*Pssst,*" whispered Pizza Pete, the manager of the Pizza Piehole. "I can get you out of here!"

He poured tomato sauce over SpongeBob's hands, and they slipped out of the chains. But then he tied SpongeBob's wrists together with a garlic breadstick.

"You're coming to cook for me," Pizza Pete said. "My customers can't get enough of your Pizza Patties!"

When SpongeBob got outside, he was grabbed by the manager of the Wet Noodle. "I'll take one fry cook to go!" the manager shouted.

They didn't get far before Señor Taco from Taco Sombrero snatched SpongeBob.

All the managers wanted SpongeBob to work for them.
They chased and clutched and pulled at him.
"Help!" SpongeBob cried.

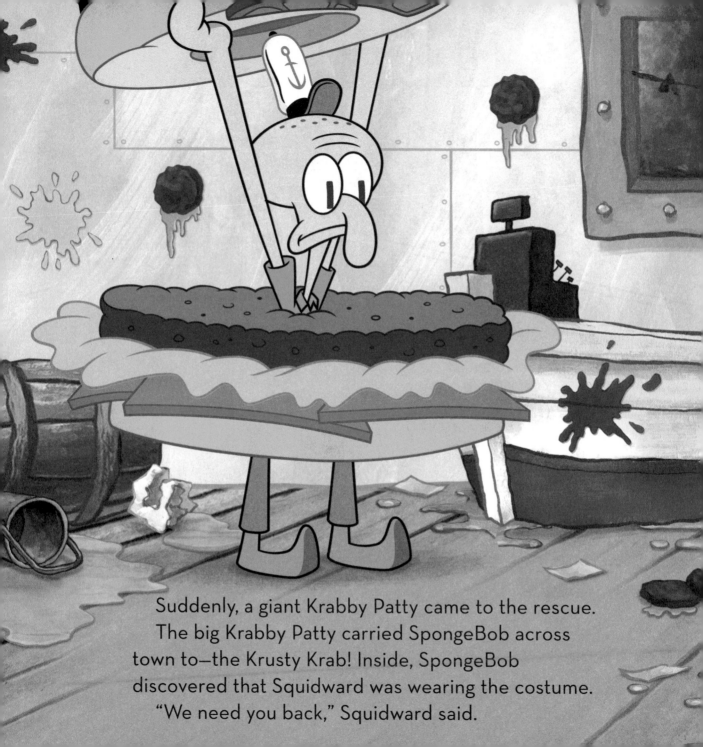

Suddenly, a giant Krabby Patty came to the rescue. The big Krabby Patty carried SpongeBob across town to—the Krusty Krab! Inside, SpongeBob discovered that Squidward was wearing the costume. "We need you back," Squidward said.

"Laddy, I should never have let you go!" cried Mr. Krabs. "This place is a wreck without you. I'm hiring you back, SpongeBob." SpongeBob looked around. The tables were messy, smoke poured from the kitchen, and sauce dripped from the walls. "My life has purpose again," he said with a sigh.

While SpongeBob was busy working, he noticed something strange about the bathroom door.

"It's a pay toilet," Mr. Krabs explained. "That's how I'm making up the nickel I lose by hiring you. You're worth it."

SpongeBob had never been happier to be at work.